Hi! I'm Dink, the Tooth Fairy.

I've taken a short break from collecting gorgeous baby teeth from under pillows, to write you this little guide to fairies. Enjoy!

Who are we?

Fairies are magical creatures, who look just like human boys and girls, just much smaller. We have delicate wings like a butterfly's, so we can fly amongst the flowers, and sometimes pop in to visit little children. We are the guardians of nature and animals, and report to Mother Nature.

Most fairies are very shy which is why humans will not often see us, but occasionally we do get spotted holding hands and dancing in circles in the moonlight. Sometimes people may see us as small bright lights flittering through the woods or meadows, or dancing over ponds.
We love to dance!

What do we do?

Fairies are protectors of nature and help look after the plants, insects and small creatures. We love to help things grow. We especially love flowers, and use them to decorate our clothes and houses; we guard all plants and help them to grow: trees, bushes, herbs, fruit, and vegetables.

Did you know...
our dancing helps
the plants grow?

We love all things of beauty,
and we love having fun!
Mostly, we only come out at
night, and spend many merry
hours dancing, singing and
giggling with our friends
in the forests.

One of the things we love most of all, is spreading our joy and happiness to our human friends. When humans are kind to each other and to the earth, we bless them with our fairy magic.

When a fairy lives in your home, we can bring joy, laughter and magic (and sometimes mischief!).

When a fairy lives in your garden you can be blessed with wonderful plant growth and lots of luck.

Where do we live?
Fairies live in Fairyland which is magical and mysterious, and can't be seen by human eyes.
It is a land where time doesn't exist, so we never grow old and live forever.

There are many different types of fairies, and each has their own favourite place to make their home. Some fairies live underground, some fairies live in trees, some in the sea, and some in the sky. Flower fairies and butterfly fairies are the ones most likely to be found in your gardens, living among the flowers and near the bottom of trees.

Flower Fairies

These are peaceful and playful little folk, who love beauty and luxury. They love to be surrounded by all things of nature and to wear beautiful flowers. Flower fairies love to make friends with human children, especially those who are kind and look after the earth.

Butterfly Fairies

These are shy and delicate fairies, who have beautiful coloured butterfly wings. They love to dance with Monarch butterflies. They do not trust humans, who have been destroying their forest homes, and tend to hide in dark, mossy areas. However, Butterfly Fairies can become true friends for life and bring you good luck.

Woodland Fairies

Woodland Fairies are happy, loyal creatures who love to make friends and to hear your dreams and wishes. They are simple creatures who want nothing more than to share their gifts and happiness. Your acts of kindness revitalise their power, keeps them happy and makes them feel welcome.

Star Fairies

Star Fairies are kind and devoted creatures, who value true friendship. To help ease your problems, they take everything in your heart into their heart. They love nothing more than to grant your wishes.

Golden Fairies

These fairies are outgoing, energetic and cheerful (and can be rather mischievous). They love to party with their many fairy friends. Golden fairies love to entertain and to share their gifts of confidence and courage.

Wood Elves

Wood Elves live deep within forests and protect the earth: the soil, plants, trees, insects and animals. They are nimble and can move so fast through the forests, humans may only just catch a glimpse of their shadow. They are trustworthy and fair, and make great listeners and companions.

How do you invite a fairy to stay?
Fairies are secretive and prefer to keep
out of the way of humans, so if you
would like to invite one of us to live in
your home or garden, you will first
need to earn our trust and respect.
If you are kind to wildlife and take
an interest in helping the planet,
we will be impressed.

We are most attracted to:
* Plants, flowers and trees
* People who love nature
* Imaginative children
* Shiny, sparkly objects
* Laughing

Things we don't like:
* Loud, clanging wind chimes
* Loud Bells
* Rude children
* Laziness
* Lots of clutter and mess

There are three ways to invite a fairy to stay with you:
* Displaying a fairy door
* Making a fairy house
* Creating a fairy garden

Fairy Doors

Fairy doors provide a magical
entrance from our fairy realm
into your world.

Once your door is put up,
we will know we are welcome
to come to stay with you.

If you would like to invite a fairy to live in your home, you can put up your door inside – perhaps on a skirting board, a wall, door or window. If you would prefer one of us to watch over your garden, you could place your door on a tree, wall, fence or gate.

We don't like clutter and mess, so you may need to clean and tidy your room to attract a fairy to your home. House fairies can be very helpful and playful. Sometimes they may play silly pranks like moving or hiding things, but mostly they will bless your home and bring you good luck.

Fairy Houses

Another way to show the fairies that they are welcome to come to stay, is to make a special fairy house for us to live in. Fairy houses can be bought ready-made or they can be made by you.

Fairy houses provide a place for us to play and rest; our very own little home, with a small door to come and go. We love our homes to be made of natural materials and decorated with all the wonderful things found in our natural outdoor habitat: moss, grass, acorns, shells, twigs, feathers, berries, pinecones, nuts, and bark.

We also love bright colours, sparkles, shiny things and interesting keepsakes. We love to decorate our homes with lots of shiny objects, many that we may have 'borrowed' from inside your house!

Fairy Gardens

To entice a fairy to come to stay in your garden, you may want to create a space that's just for us, where we can feel safe and welcome. We are very small so we only need a small space to call our own.

Fairies are attracted to natural beauty, flowers and plants. Growing scented plants liked herbs and flowers, and plants that attract insects, bees and wildlife, will also be attractive to us. We are creatures of nature, and enjoy places that bring together the elements of earth (soil), water, fire (sun) and air.

Fairies like little pools of water and wind chimes, but we are frightened away by fountains and bells. We love lots of secret nooks to hide away, and things to excite our curiosity, things to play with and places to explore.

How will you know a fairy has arrived? Your fairy guest may leave you a note, but the most likely telltale sign that a fairy has moved in is when little things seem to be out of place or missing. As hard as we try, we just can't help being mischievous!

You may see a sparkle trail where we have flown, or if you come across a small pile of sparkles, that means you startled your fairy, who was just seconds away from being seen.

Once a fairy has moved in with you, they will keep your pets happy, watch over your house and garden, tend to the plants, and bring good luck.

How can you keep your fairy happy?
Fairies love to be left little gifts
or offerings, such as:

* Leaving out food, for example, bread, milk, honey, cakes or sweets
* Leaving gifts of natural objects you have found, such as flowers or shells
* Leaving gifts of arts and crafts you have made
* Reading stories, playing music or singing
* Writing us a letter, poem or story
* Laughing and playing — we love people having fun so we can join in!

The Fairy Code

Be a friend to the fairies
Be kind to all creatures
Show courage and try your best
Keep neat and tidy
Look after plants and insects
Be generous and helpful to others
Be polite and well mannered
Be imaginative and creative
Have fun and share your smiles
Count your blessings

I hope you enjoyed my little book, and will soon have your very own fairy living with you.

ps. Don't forget to keep those teeth sparkly clean!

Fairy Wonderland

www.MerryElfmas.com

Printed in Great Britain
by Amazon